Adapted by **STEVE BEHLING**

Based on the teleplay "Rusty's Rex Rescue"
by Andy Guerdat

Illustrated by **NATE LOVETT**

 A GOLDEN BOOK · NEW YORK

One sunny day in Sparkton Hills, Ruby and Rusty were getting ready to play a game of soccer.

"All right, show me what you've got, Rusty!" Ruby shouted as their mini robot helpers, the Bits, cheered from the stands.

Ruby was the goalie. Nobody was going to score a goal while *she* was there!

Rusty grinned. "I'll show you exactly what I've got, Ruby!"

"Presenting the one and only Kick-o-Matic 3000!"
Rusty announced.

THUMP! THUMP! They heard heavy footsteps.
The sound grew closer and closer!

At last Ruby could see the Kick-o-Matic 3000,
and it was . . . a large pair of robot legs!

"Okay, nice and easy now," said Rusty.
The Kick-o-Matic 3000 pulled a leg back
and kicked the soccer ball at the goal . . .

. . . past Ruby, through the goal, and right out of the soccer field! The machine had kicked the ball so far, nobody could see it anymore!

"I might need to make a few adjustments," said Rusty.

Ruby's robotic dog, Bytes, ran after the ball. He loved to play fetch!

A moment later, Bytes returned. He had the soccer
ball in his mouth, but it looked a lot . . . flatter.
"Hey, Bytes found the ball!" said Ruby.
"Good fetch, Bytes!" Rusty called.

Bytes raced excitedly around the soccer field with the deflated ball.
He crashed right into the Kick-o-Matic!
"Oh, no!" Ruby gasped. "Bytes, be careful!"
"It will take more than a little dent to break the Kick-o-Matic 3000!"
Rusty smiled. "Let's go, Kick-o-Matic!"
But the Kick-o-Matic did not go. It only sparked and sputtered.

BONK!

"You know what I always say!" said Rusty. "There's nothing broken that can't be fixed." Rusty opened the side panel on one of the Kick-o-Matic's giant legs.

"Here's the problem," he said. "A burnt-out microchip."

Rusty and Ruby headed back to the Rivet Lab to fix the Kick-o-Matic. But before they could start on repairs, their friend Liam stopped by.

"Hey, guys!" Liam said. "Check this out!"

Liam pulled out a toy Tyrannosaurus rex and pushed a button on it. The toy dinosaur roared!

"His name is Tyrannosaurus Ralph," Liam said proudly. "Want to play with him?"

Rusty smiled. "That sounds like fun, buddy, but right now we have some fixing to do!"

"Can I help?" asked Liam. "Can I? Can I? *Pleeeeease?*"

"Can you keep Bytes busy while we fix the Kick-o-Matic?" asked Ruby.

Liam was already running with Bytes. "I can do that! Let's go, Bytes!"

Liam and Bytes ran into the Recycling Yard.
It was full of all kinds of spare parts.
"Okay, Bytes," Liam said, looking around.
"Let's find something to play fetch with!"
Bytes wagged his tail and barked.
"You won't believe how far I can throw stuff!"
said Liam.

Bytes whined and stared at Liam, waiting to fetch.

"All you have to do is wind up . . . look at the target . . . and throw!" Liam threw Tyrannosaurus Ralph as far as he could. The toy sailed high into the air, and Bytes chased after it.

"See, I told you I can throw stuff," said Liam. But then he realized he had thrown Ralph a little too far. . . .

"Tyrannosaurus Ralph!" Liam yelled as he ran after the toy dinosaur. He could hear its tiny dinosaur roar, so he followed the sound to a tall tower of tires.
"Ralph?" Liam cried out. "Where are you?"
Bytes barked, looking at the top of the tire tower.

"Is he up there?" Liam asked Bytes.
Bytes barked again.
Sure enough, peeking at them from
the tippy-top tire was Tyrannosaurus Ralph!
"Hang on, Ralph!" Liam called.
"I'll save you!"

Liam saw that the tower of tires was very wobbly. But next to the tires was a big pile of junk. Liam started to climb up the pile.

And climb.

And climb.

Soon he had nearly reached the top. He looked over at the tires. He could see Tyrannosaurus Ralph!

Without thinking twice, Liam jumped from the junk pile to the tire pile.

"Whoa!" he gasped as the tire stack teetered. He grabbed Tyrannosaurus Ralph. "Sorry for tossing you up here." He gave the toy dinosaur a huge hug. "Still friends?" He pressed Tyrannosaurus Ralph's button, and the dino roared happily.

Down below, Bytes barked anxiously.
"This is way higher than I thought," said Liam. He was worried. He looked over the edge of the top tire. . . .

Liam felt like he was up in the clouds and the Recycling Yard was a million miles below. How was he going to get himself and Tyrannosaurus Ralph down?

CREAK!

"That's not good!" said Liam when he heard the sound.
The nearby junk pile started to shake.
It started to shimmy.
It started to—

RUMBLE!

Meanwhile, back at the Rivet Lab, Rusty and Ruby were hard at work fixing the Kick-o-Matic.

Ruby put the brand-new microchip in place. "And . . . done!" she said.

"Now for the tricky part," replied Rusty. "How about some light, Ray?"

Ray shined his light so Rusty could see better.

Rusty took a good look at the microchip panel.

"Crush?" he asked. "Screwdriver!"
Crush cruised over with the tool.

"Whirly? Pliers!" said Rusty.
Whirly flew in with the pliers.

"This sure is thirsty work." Rusty wiped his brow. "You know
what I could use? Chocolate milk!"
With his lift arm, Jack gave Rusty a carton of chocolate milk.

Rusty finished his chocolate milk and went back to his repairs. "Now for the finishing touch," he said. "And I have to be careful. One wrong move—"

RUMBLE! CRASH!

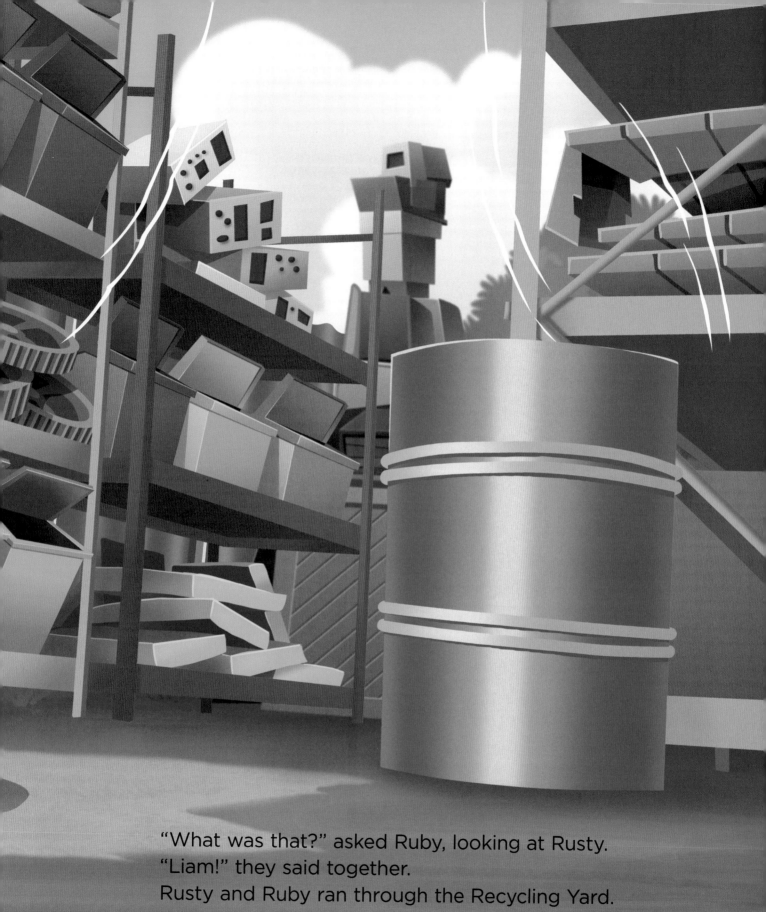

"What was that?" asked Ruby, looking at Rusty.
"Liam!" they said together.
Rusty and Ruby ran through the Recycling Yard.
"Liam, where are you?" called Ruby.
They didn't see any sign of Liam or Bytes, so they kept running, and they kept looking.

Suddenly, they heard Bytes barking. Rusty and Ruby followed the sound all the way to the tower of tires.

"Bytes!" said Rusty. "Where is Liam?"

Bytes whined and looked at the top of the tower.

"Liam!" Rusty and Ruby shouted.

"Hi!" Liam croaked.

Rusty and Ruby had to think fast. How were they going to get Liam down?

"I know!" said Ruby. "Let's get some Bits on the fix!"

Ruby pulled out her tablet and called their mini robot friends.

They would need **CRUSH** . . .
and **WHIRLY** . . .
and **RAY** . . .
and **JACK**, too!

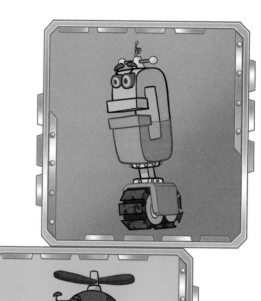

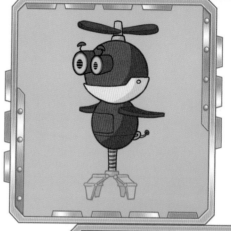

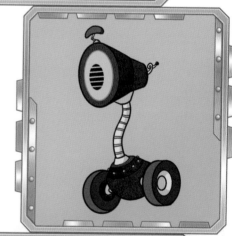

Ruby, Rusty, and the Bits worked together, standing on top of each other to form a ladder. But they just weren't tall enough! "A little higher, Jack!" called Rusty.

Jack tried to go higher, but he couldn't.

"Reach, Crush!" called Rusty.

Crush tried to reach.

"I don't think this is going to work," said Rusty.

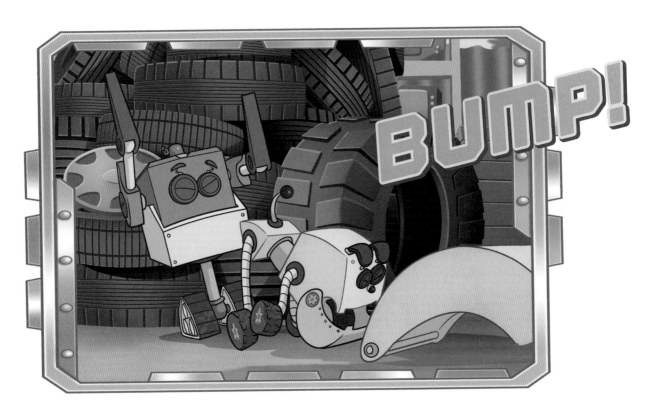

Bytes wanted to help. He grabbed a big metal scoop and dragged it over to his friends.

Bytes accidentally bumped the big scoop into his friends. One by one, they tumbled to the ground!

"We can't play fetch right now," Ruby said to Bytes. "Besides, that scoop is way too big. We'd need a giant magnet to lift it."

"That's it!" said Rusty. "We can use the magnet crane!"

The magnet crane could reach high places. Maybe it could reach the top of the tall tower of tires!

Rusty and Ruby ran for the crane.

"Time to bolt!" cried Rusty as he started up the magnet crane.

"This way!" shouted Ruby. She guided the magnet crane over to the tower of tires. Because there were pieces of scrap metal everywhere from the fallen junk pile, the crane had to move very slowly.

"Oh, no!" said Ruby. "The crane is too wide to fit through all the junk!"

Ruby was right. There was too much scrap metal. The crane couldn't get close enough!

"You guys better hurry," Liam shouted down.
"Ralph is super-duper scared!"
   Rusty and Ruby looked up at Liam and Ralph.
The toy dinosaur gave them an idea.
   "Ralph!" said Rusty. "That's it! Let's combine it—"
"—and design it!" finished Ruby.

Rusty pressed a button on his glove, and blueprint designs appeared in the air.

"We have to get Liam down with something that's tall but not too scary," Rusty said.

He looked around the Recycling Yard. There were old car parts everywhere.

"If we start with car parts . . . ," Rusty began.

". . . and we use the Kick-o-Matic's super-tall legs . . . ," added Ruby.

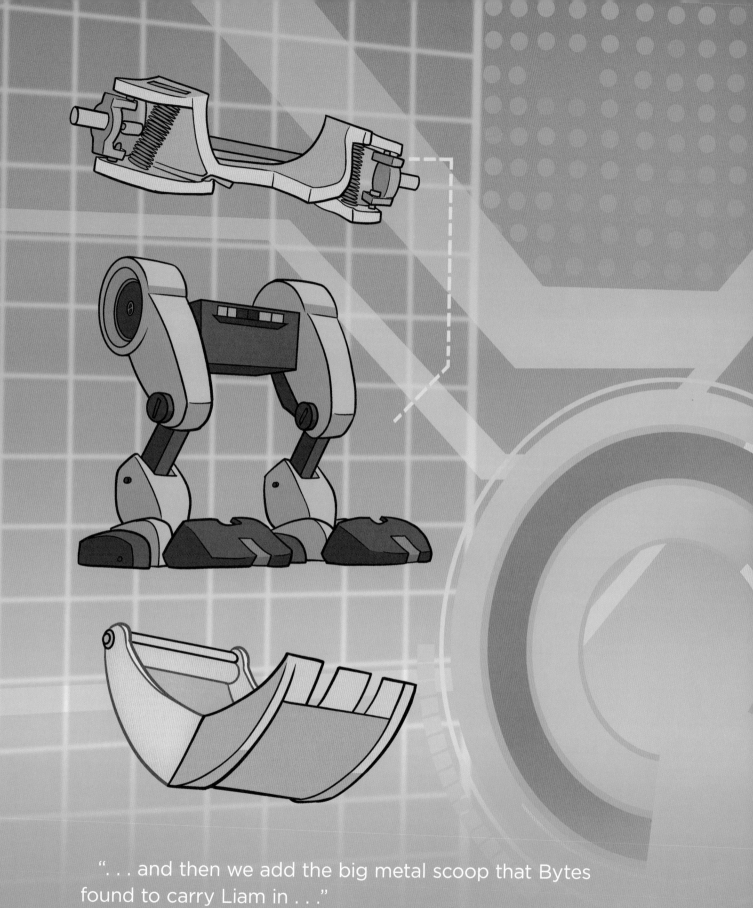

". . . and then we add the big metal scoop that Bytes found to carry Liam in . . ."

On the blueprint, all the pieces came together.

"Put it all together, and we've got our plan!" said Rusty.

Rusty and Ruby started to build. The Bits helped, too!
They tested the legs on the Kick-o-Matic. It was
moving better than ever!
Then they added car parts and the big metal scoop,
and the rescue machine began to take shape.
Rusty smiled. "Modified. Customized. Rustified!"
The machine was finished! But what had they built?

"The one, the only—the Botasaur!" announced Rusty, pointing at the enormous Tyrannosaurus rex robot they had just made.
"Let's see what he can do!"
Botasaur gave a mighty roar. The roar was so loud, it blew the Bits over!
"Let's try something a little safer," said Ruby with a chuckle.

Ruby tapped away on her tablet.
Suddenly, the Botasaur meowed!
Bytes heard the sound and ran over. The Botasaur was afraid of Bytes. Bytes barked and began to chase the giant robot!
"Cute, but maybe a little too cute," said Rusty.
"I think I've got it!" said Ruby. She pressed some buttons on her tablet.

Now the Botasaur started to behave like a dog! It stuck out its tongue, panting. It wagged its tail. Bytes wagged his tail, too. He was happy to have a big Botasaur playmate!

"Twice the puppy, twice the fun!" said Ruby.

"All right, Botasaur!" shouted Rusty. "Let's go save Liam!"

Rusty and the Botasaur dashed off. Ruby, Bytes, and the Bits rushed after them.

The Botasaur's loud stomping startled Liam. He couldn't believe what he was seeing—an enormous metal Tyrannosaurus rex!

"Are you Ralph's daddy?" he asked in wonder.

Rusty peeked out from behind the Botasaur.

"Hey, Liam!" he called. "Need a lift?"

The Botasaur raised his enormous head to the tippy-top of the tall tower of tires.

"Hop in!" called Rusty.

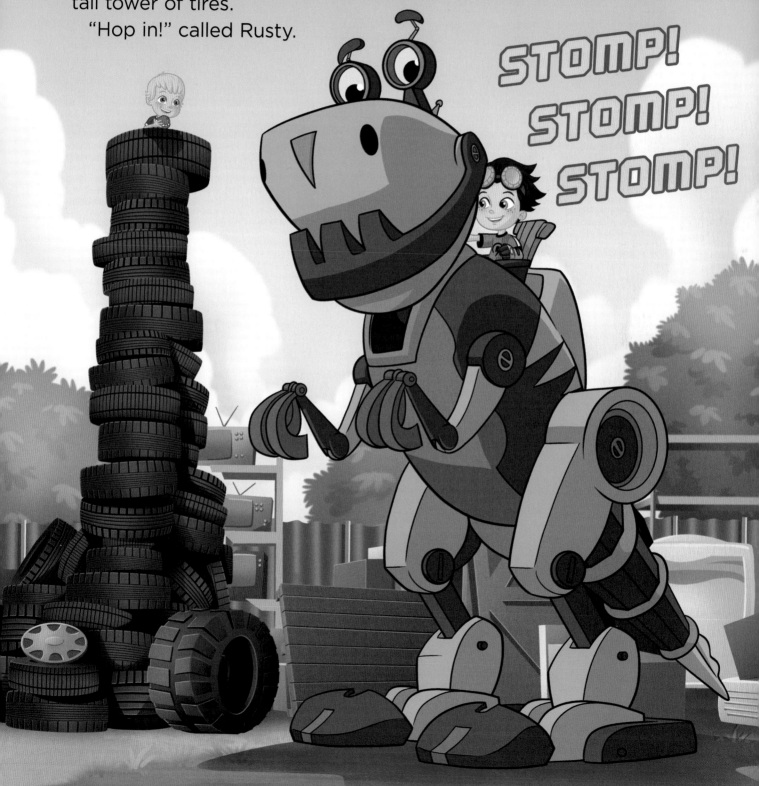

STOMP! STOMP! STOMP!

Holding tightly to Ralph, Liam climbed inside the Botasaur's mouth. The big dino lowered its head to the ground, and Liam jumped out.

"We did it!" said Ruby. "Way to go, Botasaur!"

"Thanks, Botasaur!" said Liam. "Ralph has something he'd like to say, too."

Liam pressed the button on his toy dino, and it let out a tiny roar.

"That means 'thank you' in Dinosaur," he said.

Rusty laughed and smiled up at the Botasaur.

Not only had they fixed the problem, but they had also built a great new friend!

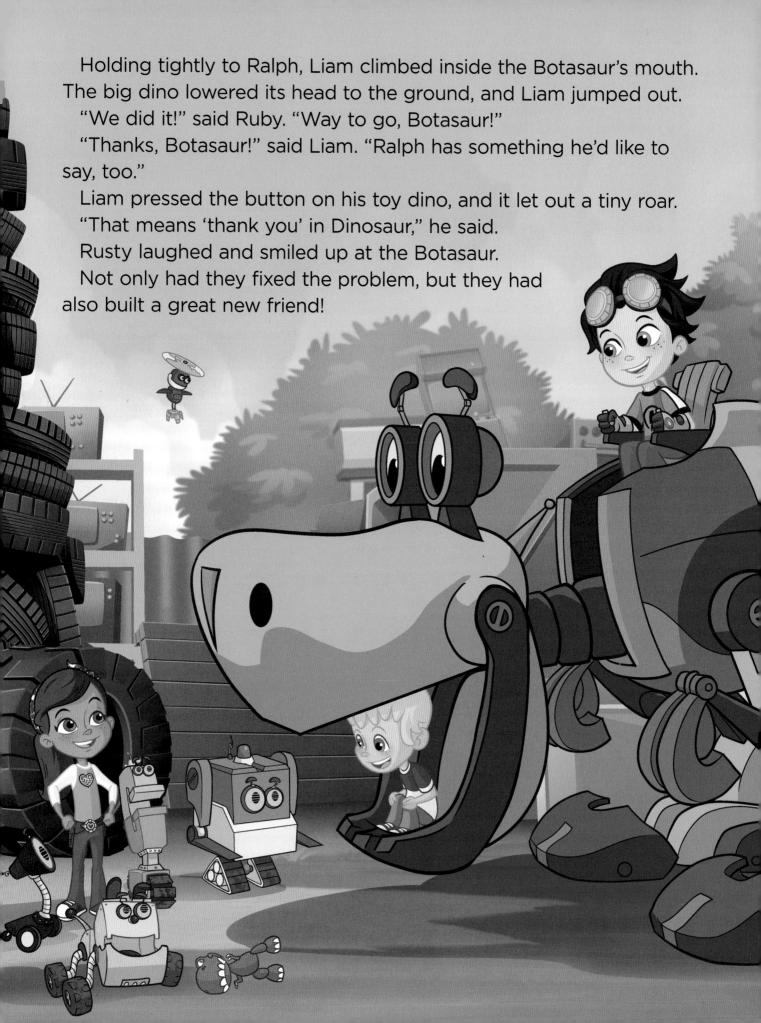